My Amazing Toddler
Behavioral Series

I Use My Words.
I Speak UP!

By Suzanne T. Christian

TWO RAVENS
BOOKS

Two Little Ravens
CHILDREN'S NON-FICTION BOOKS

Paperback Edition: 9781964202082
Hardcover Edition: 9781964202099
Digital Edition: 9781964202105

Published in the United States by Two Ravens Books LLC,
254 Chapman Rd, Ste 209, Newark DE 19702

'Expand the mind, free the imagination, one title at a time.'
www.tworavensbooks.com

Welcome to
"I Use My Words. I Speak Up!"

This book is a delightful collection of easy-to-understand affirmations designed specifically for young children. As you explore its pages together, your child will learn the importance of communication, confidence, and assertiveness.

Each page features vibrant illustrations and relatable scenarios that encourage the positive expression of feelings and thoughts. By making this book a regular part of your reading routine, you can witness a gradual improvement in your toddler's communication skills, as repetition is a proven teaching tool.

Prepare for a journey of verbal growth, confidence, and lots of fun with your toddler!

Suzanne T. Christian

Saying "Hello" makes new friends!

When I see something fun, I say, "Look!"

Asking **"What's that?"** helps me learn new things.

When I need help, I say, **"Help, please!"**

"Please" and "Thank you" and are my magic words

I say "**No thank you**", when I don't want something.

Asking **"why"** helps me discover new things.

I say **"Snack please"**,
when I am hungry.

"More please,"
gets me what I need.

When I need to go potty, I say, **"Potty please"**

"All done!"
tells Mommy.
I'm finished.

"I'm sorry",
helps make things better.

I say, **"Hug Please,"**
when I feel sad.

I tell my pet, **"Good boy!"** to make them happy

"Let's share," makes games more fun.

"Goodbye," means I'll see you later.

When I say **"I love you"** it makes everyone smile.

When I'm tired,
I say,
"I need a nap."

I use my words.

I Speak up!

The End!

My Amazing Toddler Behavioral Series

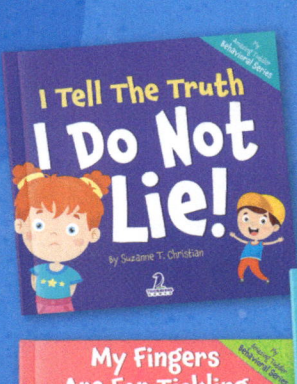

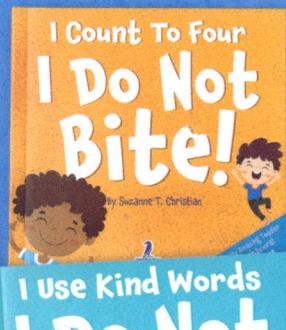

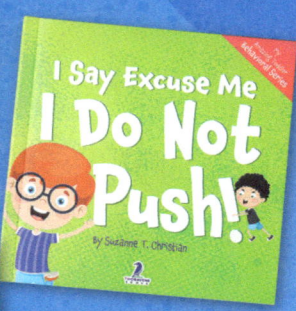

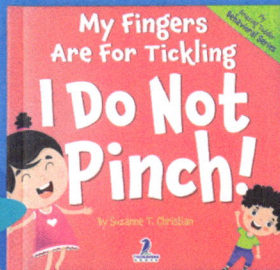

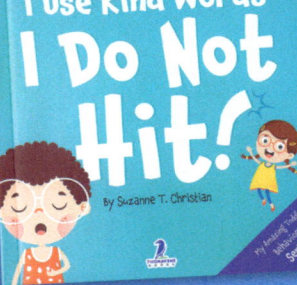

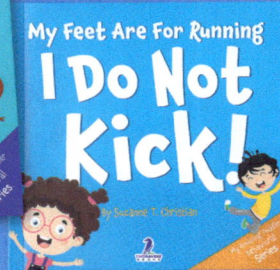

Check Out
Suzanne T. Christian's beloved series
'My Amazing Toddler Behavioral Series'.
Young readers are sure to enjoy!

Two Little Ravens
CHILDREN'S NON-FICTION BOOKS

Dear Amazing Reader,

Thank you for diving into **I Use My Words. I Speak Up!** with me. If this book touched your heart or made a difference for a young reader, I'd be grateful if you could share your thoughts in a review. Your feedback inspires my future work and helps others discover the magic within these pages.

I'd love to hear from you directly if you have suggestions or ideas for improving the book. Please feel free to reach out to me at **suzanne.christian@tworavensbooks.com.** Your voice counts, and I cherish it deeply.

With heartfelt gratitude,

www.ingramcontent.com/pod-product-compliance
Lightning Source LLC
Chambersburg PA
CBHW041600120626
46551CB00002B/271